Utterly Flutterly Fairies

Sophie
the
Birthday Fairy

Utterly Flutterly Fairies

Sophie
the
Birthday Fairy

Moira Butterfield

Illustrated by Liz and Kate Pope

Potter
BOOKS

Freya's home

Daisy's home

Human School

Fairy Sch...

Clara's home

Windmill Wood

Human town

rubbish

Seashell Beach

Meet the Utterly Flutterly Fairies!

Sophie the Birthday Fairy

Special spells in her backpack

Clever weather magic dust
The power to conjure up some sunshine

Magic beauty jewel
The power to make someone hear beautiful music

A good feeling spell ring
The power to put a smile on someone's face

Sophie's special skill
*She is especially good at looking after animals,
and can talk their languages*

Clara the Clever Fairy

Special spells in her backpack

Clever weather magic dust
*The power to create a gentle breeze
(No wonder her Dad is always
inventing new kinds of windmill
to help run their home)*

Magic beauty jewel
The power to change colours

A good feeling spell ring
The power to give someone a bright idea

Clara's special skill
*She can make objects move a little (she's still
learning how to make them move a lot). She
can also magically see where things are broken*

Freya the Fashion Fairy

Special spells in her backpack

Clever weather magic dust
The power to make a rainbow

Magic beauty jewel
The power to create beautiful clothes

A good feeling spell ring
The power to give someone a happy thought

Freya's special skill
*She is able to camouflage herself,
so people don't see her*

Daisy the Dream Fairy

Special spells in her backpack

Clever weather magic dust
The power to calm storms

Magic beauty jewel
The power to create starlight

A good feeling spell ring
The power to make everything taste dreamy

Daisy's special skill
*She is able to fly very fast
and she is good at sport*

Drizzle the Wicked Witch

*She would just love to get her hands on the fairies' spells, with
the help of her mean and horrible sidekicks, the Craggy Crows!*

More Utterly Flutterly Fun!

Look out for the pages of Utterly Flutterly Fairy Fun at the end of this book.

Make your own perfume

Recipe ideas

Organise your birthday party

Make a paper chain

Written by Moira Butterfield
Designed by Tracey Cunnell
Edited by Pat Hegarty
Illustrated by Liz and Kate Pope

Created by WizzBook Ltd
Copyright © 2009 WizzBook Ltd
All rights reserved.

First published in the UK
by Potter Books, RH17 5PA, UK

Reprinted 2009

www.potterbooks.co.uk

Printed in the UK by CPI Bookmarque, Croydon, CR0 4TD

Chapter 1
A School Surprise

The next time you go to your school, look carefully around the playground. Is there a quiet spot in a corner? Could something small, secret and magical be hiding there? I heard that in a hole in a tree, on the edge of somebody's school playground, there was a very special secret indeed – the *Utterly Flutterly Fairy School!* I don't know which playground it's in. It could be yours. If you spot it, keep it a secret, won't you?

Little fairies arrive at the fairy school every morning, just after the human children have gone indoors. Some of the fairies ride on animals, and some of them arrive on funny magical machines.

I was told this story about an especially kind and thoughtful school fairy called Sophie. She rode to school with her mum, on two fairy unicorns. Sophie had a baby one called Tiggy.

Giddy up, Tiggy!

Sophie could talk to animals. Not many fairies can do that. One morning she was feeling a little bit worried, and she told Tiggy all about it. She knew that her teacher, Mrs Daffodil, was planning a surprise lesson.

Sophie sighed. "I'm good at some kinds of magic, but what if the lesson is a really hard spell and I mess it up? Once I had to turn stones into flowers in front of the whole class. I got the spell wrong and I turned them into blue frogs. They hopped into Mrs Daffodil's pockets."

Tiggy thought that was funny, and even Sophie started to smile at the thought of frogs wriggling and tickling Mrs Daffodil.

She needn't have worried about the lesson. When she got to school Mrs

Daffodil told the fairy class what was in store, and it was a nice surprise.

"Today we are going to a top unicorn stable to learn more about riding and unicorn-care. The very finest unicorns live there."

Sophie's friend Clara the Clever Fairy grinned. "It's perfect for you, Sophie!" she said.

Freya the Fashion Fairy chuckled, too. "You can help me. I'm rubbish at riding. I'll probably get on backwards!"

Sophie got so excited that her wings wouldn't stop fluttering, and no wonder. Fairy unicorns are very beautiful, with white velvet wings and a pale coat that shines like the pearly inside of a shell. The best unicorns can fly as smoothly and cleverly as a bird.

All the fairies put on their magical backpacks ready for the trip, each with their own precious spells safely inside. They climbed on to the school bus, which wasn't really a bus at all. It was an empty bird's nest pulled along by rainbow-coloured beetles. Mrs Daffodil cast a spell on it so nobody would see them as they flew out of the tree.

"Remember, we have enemies," Mrs Daffodil warned. "Drizzle the Witch and her horrible Craggy Crows want your spells. Don't let your backpacks out of your sight."

Everyone replied together. "Yes, Mrs Daffodil!"

Mrs Daffodil waved her hand. "Off you go, bus beetles. Next stop, the unicorn stables!"

Chapter 2
King of the Unicorns

The fairy unicorn stable was in a flower meadow. There were stalls for the unicorns and a riding ring for practising. Because unicorns can fly there were also riding jumps hanging high in the branches of nearby trees.

All the school fairies had a wonderful time, but Sophie loved it there most because she could talk to the prize unicorns she met. They told her about the adventures they had had flying here, there and everywhere. She told them about Tiggy.

"He's my baby unicorn. I am still learning to ride him. I make sure he's got food and I brush him every day."

The biggest and most beautiful-looking unicorn spoke to her. "We heard you were a kind fairy, Sophie. Come back and see us whenever you like."

Sophie's friend Daisy the Dream Fairy got very excited. "Wow, Sophie! You were talking to the King of the Unicorns. He's probably flown around the whole world!"

When the fairies got back to their school it was breaktime. They sat on a tree branch chatting about their trip, being careful to stay out of sight amongst the leaves. Only, instead of feeling happy, Sophie began to feel strangely worried, and here's why.

You see, Sophie was a Birthday Fairy. They give presents to babies on their birthdays – special secret gifts such as kindness and beauty. Do you remember the story of Sleeping Beauty? When she was a baby some good fairies gave her gifts. *They* were Birthday Fairies. In fact, they were Sophie's great-aunties!

When somebody human began to feel unhappy or worried about a birthday, Sophie couldn't help feeling the same thing, because she was a birthday fairy. It made her want to help. So when she looked anxiously down from the tree and saw a sad little girl sitting all on her own, she had to do something.

She reached inside her magical backpack, and found her Good Feeling Spell Ring. Every little fairy has one, with its own special magic. Sophie's ring had the power to put a smile on somebody's face.

She slipped the ring on her finger and thought hard to make the magic work. The little girl's mouth turned up into a small smile, but only for a moment.

Sophie was shocked. "She really is *very* sad. My ring magic can't make her smile for more than a second or two. I must find out why!"

Clara frowned. "But how will you do that? You can't talk to her. It's against fairy rules."

Freya knew where the little girl lived. "I've seen her go into a gate near my house. Perhaps we could follow her."

After school, Sophie persuaded her mum to let her go home with Freya. They set off, hoping to find out more about the little girl.

They didn't know it, but they were followed! A nosy Craggy Crow had been hiding in the tree at breaktime, and he had caught a glimpse of Sophie's magic ring. He went back to Stinky Swamp, where Drizzle the Wicked Witch lived, and he told her what he had seen.

I want that ring ~ I want it NOW!

Chapter 3

The Human House

Freya's family lived in a beautiful garden, which was ideal for them because they were all Fashion Fairies, and loved pretty things. A marble statue of a lady stood in a sunny corner of the garden, and Freya's home was cleverly hidden inside the pot she was holding.

Freya's friends loved to visit her and play amongst the flowers, but today Freya and Sophie didn't have time to stop. They hurried on past, following the little girl as she walked home from school. She turned into the gate of a garden nearby and disappeared quickly inside a house. The front door shut before the little fairies could follow.

Sophie whispered to her friend. "We'll have to find another way to get in, but we'd better be careful."

Freya glanced around nervously. "This garden isn't like the one where I live. It's very shadowy and dark, isn't it? It gives me the shivers."

Sophie agreed. "I know, but we have to be brave. That sad little girl needs our help."

They flew around to the side of the house and found a window that was open, just a little way.

Freya tried to squeeze through. "The

gap's not quite wide enough."

Sophie had an idea. "We could fit easily if we took off our backpacks, but we must hide them somewhere really safe."

Freya felt doubtful, but she could see on Sophie's face how much this meant to her.

"You're right. Let's do it," she agreed. The two friends slipped off their backpacks full of spells and hid them carefully under an empty upturned flowerpot. Then, folding their wings as tightly as they could, they squeezed through the open window into the house.

Inside, they found themselves in a hallway. They could hear the murmur of humans talking, and through an open door they saw the little girl sitting with her family.

Sophie sighed. "Oh look. She's wiping away a tear. Why is she so unhappy? Come on, let's get closer and listen in."

They swooped through the door and hid amongst a pile of toys in a corner of the room.

Freya whispered. "Sit as still as you can. Then nobody'll notice us."

But Sophie's nose began to tickle. "Oh dear. I think my wings must have stirred up some dust. A…a…tishoo!" It was only a tiny fairy sneeze, but Sophie was always very polite and she put her hand up to her mouth…a big mistake!

A baby was sitting on the floor. When Sophie moved, she caught his eye. He crawled over and stretched out his little chubby fingers.

Hide!

Freya cried out, "Hide!" Quickly she used her special Fashion Fairy magic skill, and changed colour. She camouflaged herself so the baby couldn't spot her.

But Sophie was a Birthday Fairy, not a Fashion Fairy, and she couldn't change colour. She stood, helpless and frozen with fear, as the baby reached out to pick her up...

Chapter 4
Fly, Fairies!

Freya caught hold of Sophie's arm and pulled her out of reach. At the same time, she grabbed a toy doll from the floor and pushed it into the baby's outstretched hand.

"Fly up!" she urged.

Sophie watched, horrified, as the baby put the doll into his mouth.

"Oh! That could have been me!" she gasped, and took off quickly.

The two friends flew upwards and

landed on top of the curtains. Then Freya gave her friend a hug.

"Are you alright?" she asked.

"Yes, thanks to you!" Sophie nodded.

From up high, they had a good view of the little girl sitting with her mum and dad. The little girl's mum was explaining something to her.

"Do you remember, this morning I told you Gran had hurt her knee and I'm going to help her for a little while? I'm sorry, but it means we'll have to cancel your birthday party. We'll have it next year, I promise."

The little girl nodded her head. She had been dreaming of having a birthday picnic in the sunshine, with creamy sweet birthday cake and all her friends singing 'Happy Birthday' to her. But her mum had given her the news about Gran that morning, and she'd quickly realised the party idea was doomed.

"Okay, maybe next year," she sighed.

"So that's it!" Sophie declared. "I *knew* her sadness had something to do with birthdays."

Freya fluttered her wings. "Can we go now, Sophie? It's not very safe for us here."

Sophie smiled. "Let's fly back to your place. We can sit quietly in a flower bud and think about what we can do to help."

They flew back to the window, landed on the sill, and nearly fell off with fright.

"**Miaow!**"

A fat black cat slid out from behind a curtain and blocked their way out. Sophie's special Birthday Fairy skill was talking to animals, but she wished she couldn't hear this cat's nasty voice:

"I don't remember inviting you here. Are you some kind of mouse? You look a bit odd, but you'll do for a snack."

Freya didn't understand the cat's words.

"What is it saying? Is it friendly?" she asked.

Sophie hesitated, not wanting to panic her friend. "Um…er…it's a bit fed up.

Don't go too near. I'll try to persuade it to move…"

The cat's tail began lashing to and fro. It was very grumpy.

"I can't get any rest around here. First, you two weird little mice with wings interrupt my snooze, and now there's some stupid bird outside pecking at a flowerpot. I don't know who to eat first."

Sophie glanced out of the window and gasped. One of Drizzle's Craggy Crows was standing right next to the flowerpot where they had hidden their backpacks.

Miaow!

It was trying to turn the pot over to get to their fairies' spells!

Sophie begged the cat. "We've got to get outside. Please!"

But the cat stuck out its claws and hissed menacingly.

"So sorry, miceys, but there's no chance of that."

"This cat is not being friendly, is it?" Freya whispered nervously.

Sophie's voice came out as a high-pitched, frightened squeak. "No, I'm afraid it isn't. It *definitely* isn't!"

Chapter 5
Nice Kitty!

Sophie wished her friend Clara the Clever Fairy was with them. *She* had a Good Feeling Spell Ring with the power to give someone a bright idea, and Sophie really needed one right now. Then, out of the corner of her eye, she saw the baby crawling towards them through the doorway.

She whispered to Freya. "The cat thinks we're mice of some kind. He doesn't know we can fly. We can surprise him but we have to be quick."

Freya nodded. "I'm ready."

They held hands and Sophie counted: "One, two, three…now!"

They took off together just as the cat swiped at them with his paw. Then Sophie swooped down towards the baby.

"There's a nice kitty over there. Look at his swishy tail!" she cried. Freya grinned, realising what Sophie had in mind. She flew around the baby, too, just out of reach of his stretching hand. Between them they led him towards the cat's tail. It swung invitingly down from the windowsill and it looked just like the kind of furry toy the baby loved. He gurgled happily, grabbed it and pulled hard.

"Yeow!"

The cat screeched and leapt down from the sill to hide under a chair. Outside, the Craggy Crow heard the noise and flew off in alarm.

The two fairies sped towards the open window and slipped through the gap, out into the fresh air. They rushed over to the flowerpot and pushed it over to get their backpacks.

"Let's go home," Freya declared. "It's much calmer there. Maybe Mum will give us some rose petal cake!"

"Yum, yum! Can't wait," agreed Sophie.

But the Craggy Crow hadn't given up on his mission to steal a spell. He knew that Sophie's backpack had a glittery ring in it, the one that Drizzle the Wicked Witch wanted so badly.

As Sophie pulled the pack out from under the pot he flew down and clamped his beak on one of the straps.

"Get off! Get off!" Sophie shouted. She tugged back hard and the strap flew out of the crow's beak.

As Sophie tumbled backwards, something small and shiny slipped out from inside her backpack, but she didn't notice anything wrong.

"Home, quickly!" Freya cried, and the two friends flew away as fast as they could.

The Craggy Crow *had* noticed something. His eyes shone as brightly as the Good Feeling Spell Ring that had fallen from Sophie's bag and now lay sparkling under a nearby leaf. He picked it up in his beak and flew off to Stinky Swamp.

Chapter 6
Into Stinky Swamp

Stinky Swamp didn't get its name for nothing. It smelt of rotten eggs, slimy old cabbage and the strongest, sweatiest cheese ever, all mixed up in a pongy perfume.

Drizzle the Wicked Witch liked it smelling yucky because it kept nosy people from visiting. If anyone was ever unwise enough to go there, they soon turned around and ran the other way, partly because of the sickening whiff, and partly because of the Craggy Crows. They stood in threatening ranks, their beady little eyes glinting as they guarded Drizzle's hideout.

In the centre of the swamp the yellowy-green mud bubbled up and made gooey-sounding noises like 'gloop' and 'plop'.

That's where Drizzle had her cauldron. She flew around it, stirring the mixture inside with the handle of her broomstick as she dropped in nasty things and muttered spells to make the potion stronger.

Make this evil mixture strong,
To make lots of things go wrong!

PLOP!

GLOOP!

PLOP!

But, however much she chanted, and however many horrible bits and pieces she tossed into the cauldron, she was never content. Her magic potion mixture was never quite nasty enough.

"I need more chaos and unhappiness in the world," she would hiss. The more of that there was, the stronger Drizzle's magic potion became. Her bad magic fed on unhappiness – sucking it in like air.

"I need more muddle and mess and mix-ups!" she would scream at the Craggy Crows. "One day my potion will be strong enough to help me rule the world, and the first thing I'll do is destroy the Utterly Flutterly Grottily Rubbishy School of Fairies!"

When Drizzle was in a hissy-shouty mood (which was most of the time) the

Craggy Crows would take care to sit far away from her, in case she grabbed one of them to drop in the cauldron!

You can imagine how much she hated the Utterly Flutterly Fairies, whose spells and magic skills always made people feel happy. And you can imagine the ghastly grin that cracked across her witchy face when a crow brought her Sophie's Good Feeling Spell Ring.

"Brilliant bird!" she screeched. "Let's see what this little piece of fairy jewellery can do." She grabbed the ring, slipped it on her bent wrinkly finger and pointed it at the startled crow. Straight away his beak did something very strange. It bent into a sort of smile. Drizzle looked closely at him, then pointed her finger at a couple of other Craggy Crows who weren't quick enough to hop out of the way. They all did a silly bird version of a smile.

Drizzle sniggered. "So, this ring makes everyone smile. How stupid! That's such a typical fairy trick…all cuddly and nice." She spat out the word 'nice' as if it tasted bad. "Well, let's see if we can use smiles to do mischief and make my potion stronger!"

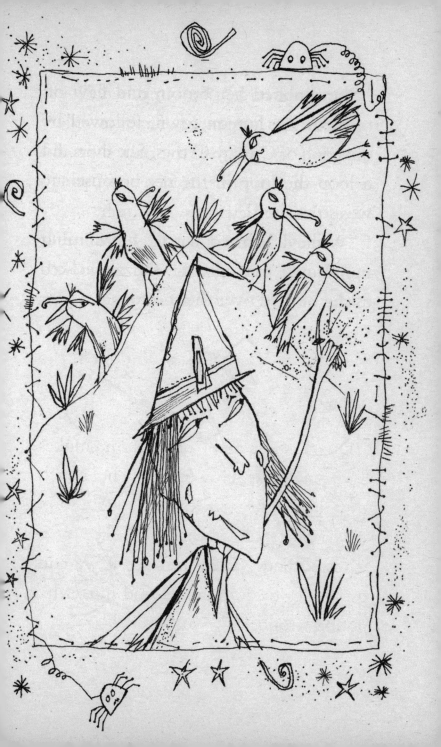

She grabbed her broom and flew off towards the human town, followed by the gang of Craggy Crows. She even did a loop-the-loop in the sky because she was so excited.

"Wahey! Wicked witchy fun coming up. Watch out, world!" she screeched, as she hurtled over the rooftops.

Chapter 7
Plan Needed!

Sophie didn't realise anything was wrong until the next morning, when her Utterly Flutterly School class went back to the unicorn stables for another lesson. Sophie and her friends were in the stables, helping to brush the King of the Unicorns' beautiful coat, when they heard a crowd of birds land in the field outside. The birds were twittering loudly as if something had upset them.

Clara glanced at Sophie, knowing

she could understand animals. "Can you hear what they are saying?" she asked.

Sophie went outside to find out what the fuss was about. When she returned she looked very pale, and her friends gathered around her anxiously.

"What is it?" Freya asked. Sophie didn't answer straight away. She slipped off her backpack full of special spells and checked inside. Then she let out a great big gulping sob.

"I knew it! My Good Feeling Spell Ring is missing, the one that makes people smile," she cried. "Drizzle has it! The birds say there's chaos in town, and it can only be her doing. The humans are all smiling madly at each other and they can't stop."

"But I don't understand. How can smiling cause chaos?" Daisy asked.

Sophie explained between sobs. "Well… sob…apparently, if humans smile when they're not supposed to…sniff…other humans get upset. Drizzle has been flying around causing accidents, you see, like sticking out her broomstick for people to trip over, or getting the Craggy Crows to splatter people with bird poo. Then she's making other people smile at the accidents as if they're pleased. The humans get angry and start shouting, and it's all my fault!"

Daisy shook her head. "Who would have guessed that smiling could be such a problem?"

Sophie wailed, "Drizzle the Wicked Witch, that's who!" She sat with her head in her hands. "I'll have to tell Mrs Daffodil. She's going to be *so* angry with me."

The King of the Unicorns gave Sophie a kindly nudge with his nose.

"Sophie, we unicorns will do all we can to help you get your ring back. Can anyone think of a plan?"

"Yes, I think I can!" grinned Clara. "I am a Clever Fairy, after all. Making plans is one of my favourite hobbies. If this one works we won't need to tell Mrs Daffodil anything." She turned to Daisy the Dream Fairy.

"Daisy, you're good at acrobatics and sport, and Sophie, you're good at riding, right?"

The mystified fairies nodded.

"Then get ready for the ride of your lives!" Clara winked.

Chapter 8
Race On!

Clara delved into her backpack and took out *her* Good Feeling Spell Ring. It had the special power of putting a good idea into someone's head. She went up behind Mrs Daffodil in the stable yard and pointed the ring at her.

"Gather round, everyone," Mrs Daffodil announced. A bright thought had just popped into her head.

"I'd like two fairies to ride together on the biggest unicorn. Sophie, you're good at riding. Take Daisy with you for a flight around the fields, but don't be too long."

The King of the Unicorns stepped up, and the two little fairies climbed on his back.

"Ready?" he asked.

"I think so," Sophie smiled nervously.

He rose smoothly into the sky.

"Wow!" Daisy grinned.

"Hold on tightly!" Sophie warned as they sped upwards. They could see their classmates below, and Mrs Daffodil signalling anxiously for them not to go too high. Then the stables disappeared as they swooped over the treetops towards the town.

As they neared the town buildings they saw a flock of crows in the sky, swarming like black flies. When they flew closer they saw Drizzle the Wicked Witch hidden amongst them.

"Oh! There she is!" Sophie gasped, suddenly feeling very afraid. Daisy gave her a reassuring squeeze.

"Don't worry. This will be fun. You ride and I'll do the rest. Fly in as close as you can."

"Okay," Sophie cried, and she patted the King of the Unicorns on the neck. "Your Majesty…let's go!"

He swooped towards the crowd of crows, scattering them with his flashing hooves and wide wings. Then he flew up behind Drizzle on her broomstick. They could see the ring on her finger.

She was flying over the park, pointing her finger at some humans arguing below.

"Why are you smiling? I fell in the pond and that's not funny!" one person was shouting.

"I don't know why," another person replied, grinning crazily.

As Drizzle concentrated on the unlucky humans, Sophie, Daisy and the unicorn flew alongside her, going so fast that the wind whistled in their ears. Daisy stretched out, holding onto the saddle with just one hand...

WHOOSH!

The unicorn hurtled past Drizzle's broomstick, as close as he could go without crashing into it. Daisy grabbed the surprised witch's outstretched finger. She pulled hard and almost fell backwards as the ring slid off. She grabbed hold of the saddle and just managed to steady herself.

"Aaargh! Come back right now!" Drizzle screamed.

The humans looked up, puzzled at the noise, but just missed the amazing sight of a witch, a unicorn and two fairies in flight, as the King of the Unicorns swooped upwards into a cloud, followed by Drizzle and her crows.

Drizzle began to catch up with the fairies.

"You're finished!" she screeched.

"Hmm, I think it's the other way round. YOU'RE finished!" Sophie grinned. "Slow down now, Your Majesty!" she cried and pulled on the reins.

The King of the Unicorns thrust his heels and wings forward and slowed his speed, taking Drizzle by surprise. As the witch zipped helplessly by, Daisy reached out and flipped the back of her broom upwards.

The broom tipped, and hurtled towards the ground. The stupid Craggy Crows followed it down, and just managed to stop themselves from crashing into the town rubbish dump below. Drizzle wasn't so lucky. She ended up buried in a pile of rotting rubbish, her broomstick smashed into pieces.

"Well done, team!" Daisy whooped. "Now we'd better get back. Mrs Daffodil won't be pleased with us for being gone so long!"

Chapter 9
Sorry, Mrs Daffodil

With Sophie's Good Feeling Spell Ring put safely away, the humans in the town stopped grinning for no reason and went back to normal. One or two went to lie down to get over the troubles of the day. Most people decided to pretend nothing weird had happened and never mentioned it again, in case anyone thought they had gone mad.

Meanwhile, with no broomstick, Drizzle had to get her Craggy Crows to

pick her up like a piece of ragged washing
and fly her back to Stinky Swamp, where
she decided she needed a long rest away
from anyone good.

Sophie, Daisy and the King of the
Unicorns sped back to the stables to face
Mrs Daffodil, who was cross with them
for being gone so long.

"You naughty young fairies. You

shouldn't have sped off like that, to goodness knows where. I was about to come and search for you. You should know better."

"We're sorry, Mrs Daffodil," Sophie apologised, but at the same time she put her thumb up behind her back, so Clara and Freya would know that the plan had worked.

Before the fairy friends left the stables they all gave the King of the Unicorns a hug and thanked him for his help.

"Don't mention it. It was fun!" he whinnied. "You are a very good young rider, Sophie. Don't forget to tell your pet unicorn Tiggy about your flying adventures, will you? He'll be so proud of you!"

Sophie laughed. "I won't forget, and next time I ride him we'll practise swooping and slowing down, just like you do so beautifully. He'll love it!"

On the way back to school the four friends stayed quietly at the back of the beetle bus, keeping out of Mrs Daffodil's way. Sophie was quieter than everyone because she was thinking hard. Then she piped up.

"I'll need help tomorrow, everyone," she whispered. "Don't worry. It doesn't involve climbing into a house or chasing a witch! It will be the best fun, I promise."

"Okay. I'm in, as long as I don't have to meet that horrible cat again!' Freya grinned, and the others agreed.

"If that sad little girl from the house can't have a birthday party at home, then she can have one at our school," Sophie explained. "We'll use our magic to throw an Utterly Flutterly fantastic fabulous birthday party!"

Chapter 10
Party!

The next day, during their school breaktime, the fairies sprang into action. First, Clara the Clever Fairy flew onto a branch overlooking the human school playground, where she got a good view into the head teacher's office. She slipped on her Good Feeling Spell Ring, pointed her finger, and gave the head teacher a very bright idea indeed.

"One of the little girls has a birthday today. Let's have a party for her," said the head teacher, surprising herself and everyone else in the office!

Meanwhile, Freya the Fashion Fairy rummaged in her backpack and found a pretty jewel – her Magic Beauty Jewel. Each of the fairy friends had a different one, and Freya could use hers to magically create beautiful clothes. She used it to put a party outfit into every child's school bag.

Daisy the Dream Fairy wasn't to be outdone. After all, she had a Good Feeling Spell Ring, too. It gave her the power to make food taste dreamy. She made the children's lunches taste like the yummiest party food ever, and gave them all a piece of creamy soft birthday cake.

Finally, Sophie opened her backpack

full of spells (looking carefully round this time, to make sure there were no Craggy Crows spying on her).

"Hmm, let's see. I've used my spell ring a lot recently…what else do I have in here? Ah yes. I think it's time to sprinkle some Clever Weather Magic Dust!" She waved her hand and some of her sparkly dust flew into the air. Immediately the clouds parted, the sky turned blue and the sun came out to provide perfect party weather.

"And finally I need my Magic Beauty Jewel," Sophie grinned. She could use it to make beautiful music. She picked it out from her backpack and made the 'Happy Birthday' music float magically over the playground. All the humans joined in with the song.

Happy Birthday, Happy Birthday,

Happy Birthday to you!

It was great fun to see the children enjoying themselves, but soon Mrs Daffodil rang a fairy bell to signal the end of breaktime for the Utterly Flutterly fairies.

"Job done, I think," Freya laughed, as they all went inside for their next lesson.

Sophie glanced back at the party going full-swing in the playground, and saw what every Birthday Fairy likes to see best. She didn't need to use her Good Feeling Spell Ring, that was for sure. The birthday girl already had a really big smile on her face, as her friends sang to her.

Sophie joined in under her breath, and then added a special verse of her own.

"Happy birthday to you.
Happy birthday to you.
Hurrah for Birthday Fairies,
And unicorns, too!"

Utterly Flutterly Quiz

The Utterly Flutterly Fairies all have a special way of travelling to their Fairy School. What will yours be? Find out in this Fairytastic quiz!

1. Which of the following colours do you like most?

A. *Blue and purple*
B. *Yellow and gold*
C. *White and pale pink*
D. *Gold and copper*

2. Which of these would be your favourite day?

A. *A bright spring day with lots of birds singing*
B. *A hot, sunny summer's day*
C. *A snowy winter's day*
D. *A crisp autumn day with a gentle breeze*

3. Would you like your journey to be:

    A. *Interesting, with lots to see*
    B. *Over in a flash*
    C. *Comfortable and relaxing*
    D. *Slow and gentle*

4. Which word do you like most?

    A. *Magical*
    B. *Dazzling*
    C. *Dreamy*
    D. *Golden*

5. How would you like your friends to describe your transport?

    A. *It's exciting and colourful*
    B. *It's shiny and sparkly*
    C. *It's soft and pretty*
    D. *It's beautiful and elegant*

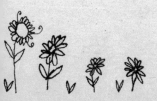

Utterly Flutterly Quiz Answers

Now check your answers to find out what your special transport would be:

Mostly As: You would soar into the Utterly Flutterly Fairy School on the back of a magnificent magical bluebird with plumes of blue and purple feathers.

Mostly Bs: You would beam into the Utterly Flutterly Fairy School on a dazzling ray of sunshine, with a trail of stars behind it.

Mostly Cs: You would float into the Utterly Flutterly Fairy School on a white fluffy snow cloud with swirls of pink marshmallow in it.

Mostly Ds: You would sweep into the Utterly Flutterly Fairy School on a giant golden leaf with glittery copper-coloured edges.

Utterly Flutterly Anagrams

Drizzle the Wicked Witch has been causing mischief by muddling up these words so that no one can read them. Can you sort them out and work out what they should say? Turn the page upside down to see if you're right.

gitgy

croniun

landrouc

kystin mwaps

serpents

eack

yarthdib trapy

pieosh

zedirlz

fyrai colohs

Birthday Fairy cakes with rose water icing!

Sophie is a Birthday Fairy so guess what she makes on people's birthdays? You've guessed it — Birthday Fairy cakes!

Ingredients for the sponge

2 large eggs
1 tsp vanilla essence
100g/4oz caster sugar
100g/4oz soft margarine
100g/4oz self-raising flour

Ingredients for the icing

100g/4oz icing sugar
1 tbs/15ml warm water
A few drops of rose water

Kit

Baking tray, fairycake paper cases, knife, sieve, spoon, two mixing bowls, wooden spoon

Sponge

1. Put all the ingredients in a bowl and beat them together until the mixture is smooth.

2. Spoon the mixture into fairy cake paper cases.

3. Bake the cakes at 180°C/350F/Gas Mark 4, for 15-20 minutes or until they are golden brown and spring back when lightly pressed.

4. Allow the cakes to cool for ten minutes. Once they have cooled down you can begin to ice them.

REMEMBER! ALWAYS ASK AN ADULT TO HELP YOU WHEN USING THE OVEN!

Icing

1. Sift the icing sugar into a mixing bowl.

2. Slowly add the water and rose water and mix until the icing is smooth and runny enough to drip from the spoon. If the icing is too thick, add more water, one drop at a time.

3. Use a spoon to drizzle some icing onto the middle of each fairy cake, and carefully spread the icing to cover the top, using a knife.

To decorate

Put a birthday candle in each cake so everyone can enjoy the birthday fun!

Fairy Tip:

You can also sprinkle hundreds and thousands or sugar strands onto the wet icing or decorate with pretty coloured icing shapes.

Throw a Fabulous Fairy Birthday Party

Would you like to throw a fabulous fairy party? Well, fairies love to play so how about a fairy game? Here are some great ideas for you:

 Fairy pass the parcel

Sleepy fairies – who can be the stillest, quietest fairy?

 Musical fairy statues

Fairy dressing-up

 Fairy treasure hunt

Fairy Picnic

How about having a fairy picnic? This can be inside or outside — all you need is a picnic blanket to spread on the ground and some party food to eat.

✳ Fairy parties are very pretty, so decorate using balloons and birthday banners. To make your party look great, sprinkle star-shaped confetti or glitter over the dinner table or picnic blanket.

✳ Why not make each guest a fairy name sticker? Take your friend's name and think of a word beginning with the same letter that describes them. You might have a friend called Lucy who is very lucky, so she could be 'Lucy the Lucky Fairy'.

✳ Write this on a sticky label and decorate with felt tip pens, glitter or sticky jewels.

Remember to give yourself a special fairy name!

Make your own rose petal perfume!

You will need:

 A handful of rose petals (around two to three roses)

 A pestle and mortar (or a mixing bowl and wooden spoon)

 A clean jar with a lid

 A sticky label

 *Colouring pens, glitter and glue*

1. Take half of the rose petals and tear them into small pieces.

2. Crush the pieces using the pestle and mortar.

3. Pour 400ml of cold water into a bowl and add the crushed rose petals to it. Stir and leave for half an hour.

4. While you're waiting, write your special fairy name on the front and decorate using pens and glitter.

5. After half an hour, sieve the mixture into a different bowl to remove the rose petals, leaving behind your fabulous fairy perfume.

6. Pour your perfume into the jar and add the rest of the petals. Stick your label neatly onto the jar and dab a drop on your wrist to smell utterly fabulous!

Fairy code words! ✦ ✦

You can make up Fairy code words by taking
each letter from a word and using it to start
another word like this:

Brilliant   **G**orgeous   **S**tunning

Interesting   **I**ntuitive   **O**bservant

Really fun   **R**eliable   **P**retty

Terrific   **L**ovely   **H**elpful

Happy   **I**maginative

Delightful   **E**ntertaining

Amazing

Yummy

More word ideas!

Why don't you try making up a fairy code word using your own name? Here are some words to get you started:

Adventurous

Determined

Wonderful

Polite

Glamorous

Beautiful

Caring

Funky

Special

Make your own fairy paper chain!

These are simple to make and look great!

You will need: *A4 paper, scissors, pencil*

1. Take some paper and fold it in half, lengthways, to make a long rectangle shape.

2. Cut down the middle line so that you're left with a rectangle.

3. Fold the paper in half and then in half again.

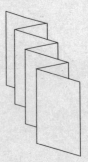

4. Copy an outline of the fairy opposite onto the front of your paper very lightly in pencil. Make sure the edges of your fairy line up with the edges of the paper.

5. Cut out the fairy shape and unfold to reveal a fabulous fairy paper chain!

Fairy Tip: make lots of paper chains and tape them together to make a fairy banner.

Look out for these
Utterly Flutterly titles!